For Rich and Juno,
who are just the way I love them.
x X x

Ingredients

A TEMPLAR BOOK

First published in the UK in 2015
by Templar Publishing,
an imprint of The Templar
Company Limited,
Deepdene Lodge, Deepdene
Avenue, Dorking, Surrey,
RH5 4AT, UK
www.templarco.co.uk

Ingredients

ISBN 978-1-78370-136-0 (hardback)
ISBN 978-1-78370-157-5 (paperback)

Edited by Libby Hamilton

Printed in China

Ciara Flood

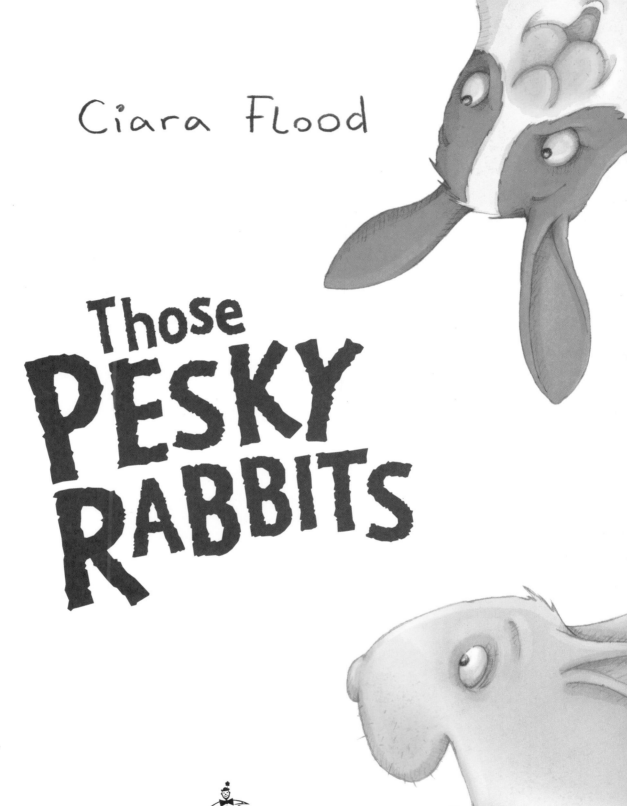

Those PESKY RABBITS

templar publishing

Bear lived on his own
in the middle of nowhere

and that was just
the way he liked it.

So, you can imagine how cross he was

when a family of rabbits
built their house

right next to his!

Soon after the rabbits had moved in there was a

KNOCK, KNOCK!

on his door.

"Hello, Mr Bear. Could we borrow some honey please? We want to bake a cake."

"I don't have **any honey**,"
Bear said.

"Pesky rabbits!" he muttered.
Bear poured himself a cup of tea,
then added a drop of milk and

**ten spoons
of honey.**

Delicious
Milk, Tea a
Hot choco

Good with figs
and Raisins

ith cheese
ers, and
grapes

Tasty w

YUMMY ON
PANCAKES

He was about to sit down when…

KNOCK,
KNOCK!

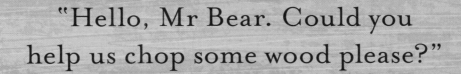

"Hello, Mr Bear. Could you
help us chop some wood please?"

"No," Bear said. "I'm far
too busy to help."

KNOCK,
KNOCK!

Bear was snoozing
in front of his fire when...

"What now?!"

he growled.

"Hello, Mr Bear.
Would you like to swap
books with us?"

Bear had just started
to eat his dinner when...

KNOCK,
KNOCK!

"Hello, Mr Bear.
Do you... wa-want to watch
sho-shooting stars with us?"

"No! No! No! No!"

Bear roared.

"What I want  is to be **left alone!"**

So that was exactly what happened.

Until one day when he heard a soft **KNOCK, KNOCK!**

But there were no
rabbits at his door,

just a basket.

Inside was a cake,
some wood, a book
and a note.

The note read:

Dear Mister Bear,

We know you have no honey to bake a cake so we've baked one for you.

yum!

We hope you can build a warm fire with the wood.

← nice and cosy

We also thought you might like to read our favourite book: THE HUTCHLIKER's GUIDE TO THE GALAXY.

↳ It's about stars, planets and space.

From,
Your Neighbours
(those pesky rabbits)

x x x x

Bear ate the cake,

made a fire with the wood

and read the book
before bed.

But he couldn't go to sleep that night.
For the first time ever Bear felt...

...lonely.

So he decided to do something he had never done before.

He went to visit his new neighbours.

Bear spent a lot of time
with the rabbits after that.

And do you
know something?

That was just the way he liked it.